The Dark Fairy

a fictional nonfiction story showing
individuals and teams how to listen and
ensure others feel understood

Nick Leja

Copyright © 2022 Nick Leja
All rights reserved.
ISBN-13: 978-0-9840250-0-8

Dedication

To us.

Acknowledgements

Thank you to the following friends for proofreading my initial manuscript and providing valuable feedback: Nick Bemiss, Laura Rief, Keith Bertram, Laura Viviano, Maria Viviano-Jurinic, Heather Petschl, Andy Weir, Alyson Weir, Christie Spudowski, and Drew Pearson. A special thanks to Lisa Arnold for dramatically helping me with vivid descriptions and interesting word choices and Kelly Viviano for supplying motivation and helping me navigate all the decisions between writing the manuscript and publishing.

Also – thank you to my dad for continuously pushing me to get back into writing and my mom for helping me see there's more to life than business.

Any wisdom you find in these pages came from reading other great authors or personal experiences with my team members, friends, and family. None of this would be possible without them.

1

I may disappear soon. In case I do, I want to write down everything I know about the Dark Fairy. Hopefully this will help you. I realize you may not be a fairy or even know what fairies are, so I'll give a brief background of us first.

Before the darkness, a large community of us lived in a mystical village. We fairies displayed the most brilliant colors, from vivid green hair to radiant purple wings. We loved colors like dogs love attention; colors made our world come alive. We used colors and imagery as a way of expressing ourselves. Just like I couldn't fully explain what the color blue looks like to you in words, we could not fully express our feelings without the use of colors, tastes, smells, and sounds.

While our wings, hair, and eyes enjoyed an abundance of color, the land around us was mostly

The Dark Fairy

dull greens and browns. Although we could fly and cast a handful of spells, we could not modify nature to make it more vibrant. At least not on our own.

Fortunately for us, there existed a special Dust that allowed us to temporarily enhance our environment in ways our own magical abilities did not allow. This Dust was found across the land, floating gently over the ground, glittering in the air whether under the midday sun or in the depth of night. When a fairy discovered Dust, they could use it to enrich the land, painting the grasses in vibrant shades of green or growing flowers that filled the air with invigorating fragrances.

Dust provoked surges of excitement throughout the village, but it was limited for two reasons. One, the effects of Dust were temporary, so whatever we created would slowly revert to how it had been before. Two, shortly after a cluster of Dust was disturbed, the unused Dust scattered and dissolved, so it had to be used as soon as it was found. Because of this, Dust created short spurts of joy rather than anything we could depend or rely on.

The Dark Fairy

Occasionally, we would discover a huge cloud of Dust that one of us couldn't use by ourselves, so we would gather our friends and family to celebrate.

We called these celebrations latías. During latías, some fairies used Dust to create exotic gardens full of brilliant hues and aromas. Others created natural streams that burbled over the ground in a soothing rhythm. Still others would dye the grass all the colors of the rainbow, shaping and cultivating it to form intricate patterns of art. Each of us had our specialty and our personal passion when it came to using Dust. One thing we all shared, however, was our love for these latías as they were a great opportunity for everyone to have fun and unwind.

One day, Caden, a curious fairy with sharp blue eyes, ivory skin, and glowing yellow wings, set out into the wilderness looking for Dust. He loved latías and wanted to find a way to make them more frequent. For years, he had worked on inventing a magic bottle he hoped would preserve Dust, allowing us to store it for later use. That afternoon, bottle in hand, he came across a clearing in the trees where the sunlight glimmered over a large cloud of Dust.

The Dark Fairy

I imagine Caden's heart raced with anticipation as he popped off the cork from his magic bottle and cast a spell, causing the Dust to rush in. When the last speck of Dust entered, he quickly slipped the cork back on, set the bottle on the grass, and sat next to it, watching it intently. After about ten minutes, Caden confirmed that the Dust inside the bottle still sparkled just as brilliantly as it always had. He had done it! He had found a way to preserve Dust!

Caden could not contain his excitement. He immediately told all of us of his new invention and showed us how it worked. He crafted as many magic bottles as he could and trained us all on how to gather and preserve Dust. Over time, he became an expert in not only how to store Dust, but also how to find it.

Because of Caden, we were able to accumulate more Dust than ever, allowing us to create ever more expressive landscapes in our village, filled with exotic colors, sounds, and smells. Because we could collect and store Dust, we could use the Dust to replenish the landscape to make our changes permanent—so long as we never ran out of it.

The Dark Fairy

As we accumulated more and more Dust, something changed within our village.

Before, finding and using Dust was a community event that brought us together. We would only interact with Dust once, maybe twice a month in any substantial way.

Now, as everyone became more focused on accumulating as much Dust as possible, fairies began hoarding Dust and only using it on the land around their homes, no longer wanting to share with others.

Latías became less frequent. Fairies became more protective of their Dust. Some even became territorial when two fairies stumbled upon the same cloud of wild Dust.

The fairies who accumulated the most Dust had the most striking landscapes, luscious gardens, rolling hills, intricate fountains, and masterful blends of colors. The other fairies looked at those landscapes with reverence, even more determined to collect more Dust to enhance their own.

The Dark Fairy

While our land became more colorful, everyone seemed sad, like something was missing. No one was happy anymore, and no one really knew why.

Caden himself seemed the most troubled of all. He used to be so eager to teach the fairies how to gather Dust, as if that brought him great fulfillment. After a while, he looked empty, like something was weighing on him. I didn't speak with him much, but occasionally, when we would make eye contact, he always looked so sad...

Many times, I saw him meeting with the village elders. I'm not sure what they spoke about, but those meetings would put Caden in the worst of moods. After them, he would frequently withdraw to his home and remain there for days before coming out again.

About a year after we started collecting Dust, Caden called the village together to discuss something. We all gathered near the village center. This was the first time we had all been gathered in months. At first, I was excited to see everyone together, but as the fairies started trickling in, I couldn't form a smile.

The Dark Fairy

Most of the fairies moved slowly and somberly, as if they were carrying an invisible burden on their backs. Typically, when we were together, we'd be whizzing back and forth in the air as we shared exciting stories or rolling in the grass as we laughed. But on this day, everyone appeared lifeless.

Once we had all gathered, Caden began speaking. He started to explain that he knew why we were all unhappy and he knew how to fix it. But in the middle of his speech, a dark magical force suddenly took hold of him. His skin turned pale, his yellow wings blackened, his eyes faded, and his voice deepened and took on a raspy tone. I had never seen anything like it. I can't explain it, but a dark aura materialized around him that seemed to control his actions and even... his thoughts.

Caden cast several seeking spells that summoned all the fairies' magic bottles to him, leaving the fairies with no more means of collecting Dust. He used that Dust to morph the ground under our village castle, a community space we used for latías and other events. The ground buckled and crumbled as a massive hill pushed up towards the sky, raising the castle higher so it overlooked the entire village.

"From this day forward," Caden declared in a deep, raspy tone, "no fairies are allowed to collect or use Dust. If you do, I will vanish you."

Caden, known from that point on as the Dark Fairy, took possession of the castle and made it his home. As he gained more Dust, he spawned skeletal, blackened trees that sprouted around the land like corpses clawing at the sky, slowly draining the surrounding area of water and life. The once beautiful environment around the village began to wither into a scorched landscape void of all colors and smells.

We fairies no longer experienced any joy. All our happiness was stripped away as we were forced to live upon the ashy land.

Since then, there have been several attempts to free the fairies from Caden's control, each attempt resulting in the fairies never coming home. Three of them, I witnessed myself.

The Dark Fairy

Attempt 1

Once, the village leader, Finn, approached the castle to speak with the Dark Fairy. Athletic, sturdy, broad-shouldered, and with determined green eyes, Finn was the most powerful fairy in the village.

Finn entered the castle and saw Caden looking out the window over the land, once vibrant with life and now darkened with sadness. Finn noticed a bottle of Dust fastened to Caden's waist.

"I wondered when you would come," the Dark Fairy said, his sunken eyes gazing out the window.

"This has gone on long enough," Finn declared. "I am the village leader. You are being selfish, cruel, and unfair to the others. I have the power to unite the others against you."

"Unfair? Is that what I'm being?" the Dark Fairy asked, still looking out the window.

"You will give us back our bottles, surrender all your Dust, and stop this madness at once."

The Dark Fairy

"Or what?" he challenged.

"Or we will rise up against you."

Caden's dark wings flickered a few times, pulling him away from the window and turning him to face Finn, his lifeless stare focusing intently on his guest.

"Spare me your empty threats. You and all the other fairies are no match for my power."

"Listen, Caden," Finn said firmly, his wings flickering more quickly as he tried to control his anger. "We have the power to—"

"Enough of this talk of power!" the Dark Fairy yelled. Cold and embittered, he flung his hand to the side, and, somehow using the darkness to weaponize the Dust from the bottle about his waist, attacked Finn with a flash of green light. Finn was never seen again.

It seemed that the darkness gave the Dark Fairy unique powers over Dust, allowing him to use it to attack other fairies, and perhaps more. This created in the rest of us a deep reluctance to oppose him.

The Dark Fairy

Attempt 2

The second attempt was from a clever fairy with long chestnut hair and purple wings named Lyla. She noticed that using threats and power to convince the Dark Fairy to give up his reign did not work, so she wanted to try a different method.

Like Finn, she fluttered into the castle, her tiny feet inches above the stone floor, and began talking with the Dark Fairy.

"What benefit does collecting all this Dust have for you?" Lyla asked. "You have enough Dust to make whatever landscapes you desire for as long as you desire."

"I'm not collecting Dust for my own satisfaction," he said.

"Then why do it?"

The Dark Fairy paused, sifting through his thoughts. A few seconds of silence passed while he considered her question, but before he answered, she continued.

The Dark Fairy

"You are collecting Dust that has no value for you, and in exchange, you are destroying your relationship with all the other fairies. Is it worth it?"

"Those relationships were destroyed long ago," he said coldly.

"But think of how they could grow again if you stopped controlling everyone and started giving back."

"I tried giving once, and that didn't work out so well."

Lyla considered his words. "What is the downside to giving them a second chance?"

"I refuse to do the same thing twice while expecting different results."

"Your relationship with others certainly won't get any worse if you release your control over them," Lyla said. *"You can't be happy living here in this castle all alone. If you continue like this, you are guaranteed to be miserable, which is the very outcome you're trying to avoid. If you give up*

control, there's at least a chance things could get better. Isn't that alone enough to make it worth it?"

The Dark Fairy shook his head and uncorked the bottle of Dust around his belt.

"There is no salvation for me," he said.

Lyla fluttered back slightly, unnerved by Caden's motions.

"Is this how you want to be remembered?" Lyla asked, trying to remain calm. "As Caden, the Dark Fairy who imprisoned his friends and neighbors? Surely you want to leave behind a better legacy than that?"

"You fairies are all the same," he said. "Always focused on what you want. Your selfishness blinds you."

"We aren't selfish, we are just trying to—"

Without waiting for her to finish, he effortlessly waved his hand, and the Dust from his bottle slithered through the air towards her. He turned around and fluttered away as the Dust coiled around Lyla's body, stealing her words and committing her to silence.

Attempt 3

The last fairy to try and convince the Dark Fairy to relinquish his power was my mother, Saya. I begged and pleaded for her not to go, but she was insistent.

My mom was an energetic and friendly fairy with big, sparkling eyes. She owned a cookie shop that made the most delicious cookies in all the land. Fairies from all over would travel to visit my mom's shop, not only for the cookies but because she was one of the kindest fairies around, always able to bring some shine to someone's day.

Before traveling to the castle, my mom baked the most flavorful cookies she'd ever created. She used the freshest ingredients to create gooey butter cookies with freshly churned chocolate, maple-roasted pecans, a dash of vanilla extract from the finest beans, and a sprinkling of cinnamon. Rather than using magic, she baked them in her special oven,

The Dark Fairy

giving the cookies a fresh, organic flavor that could not be imitated by spells.

She arranged the cookies on a platter, wrapped them in a clear film to keep them warm and moist, and flew to the castle. As she entered, she removed the film, hovered the plate across the room, and set it gently on the ground in front of the Dark Fairy.

"What's the meaning of this?" he asked.

"I can only imagine how long it's been since you've had some freshly made cookies," my mom said simply.

"If you think this will make me give you back your Dust, you're mistaken."

"I am just being kind."

"No," Caden said. "You're not. You are giving me a gift to try and manipulate me so I'll feel the need to reciprocate."

"My dear," my mom said, moving closer to him. "There are good fairies out there who want to be

kind for the sake of being kind."

"I doubt that," said Caden. "Even if you are right, it would not sway me. Now leave before you regret it."

"You poor thing. What would it take for you to trust us again?"

"That trust is gone forever."

"Come with me," my mom insisted, though deep down, I was begging for her to leave. "Come back to the village. Talk to the fairies again. It's been so long. See how they are today, not how they once were."

"I'm giving you one more chance to leave. You seem like a nice fairy, so I don't want to get rid of you like the others."

Every part of me wanted my mom to turn around and flee, but instead she moved closer.

"Please, Caden, I promise you. There are other kind fairies like myself out there. You just need to see for yourself."

The Dark Fairy

For an instant it seemed as if he wanted to agree and join her, but then the aura about him grew darker and swirled around his body faster. It was as though the darkness itself was controlling him, influencing his thoughts.

"NO!" he bellowed, and before my mom could respond, she was gone.

...

Words can't describe how I felt at that moment. My heart shattered. My mind tried to push me through that window and attack the Dark Fairy with all my might, but none of my muscles responded. I was paralyzed with grief. All I could do was collapse to the darkened grass and cry.

In the weeks after my mom disappeared, I played the events over and over in my head, trying to figure out how to stop the Dark Fairy.

I think Caden is still there, buried somewhere within the darkness. I also don't think he would actually kill any of the fairies. I'm hoping they are just prisoners somewhere within the castle. Somehow, I have to figure out how to defeat the darkness and hopefully save them.

I thought about the previous attempts to stop him. Finn tried threats, Lyla used logic, and my mom offered kindness. None of that worked. I need to try something different.

One thing I noticed is that ever since Caden turned into the Dark Fairy, some of the other fairies in the village began taking on a similar aura, though not as intense. The darker and larger their auras, the angrier and more negative they are.

While working at the cookie shop, I have interacted with several fairies that had darkness about them, and in some cases I noticed the aura would either diminish or completely vanish as we spoke. Reflecting on all those instances when the aura faded compared to when it stayed the same, I developed a theory of how to get rid of the darkness.

Iris wrote out how she planned to defeat the darkness. Her little hand ached from writing so

The Dark Fairy

much, but she wanted to get every detail on the parchment in case she did not make it back. After describing her plan, she wrote:

Today, it's time for me to put my theory to the test. Wish me luck.

-Iris

The Dark Fairy

2

Iris set her quill down on the wooden desk and rolled up the parchment scroll containing the story she'd just written. Grabbing some twine, she tied the parchment together to keep it bound in a tight roll and set the scroll at the center of her desk. She opened one of her wooden chests to reveal a small bottle filled halfway with Dust. A friend had borrowed her bottle and went exploring when Caden summoned all the bottles, sparing hers and those of a few other fortunate fairies. She strapped her bottle about her waist and made her way to the cookie shop.

Iris was a springy young fairy with glowing hazel eyes, short auburn hair, and green wings. She had been running the cookie shop ever since her mother's disappearance, longing every day for the moment when she would have the opportunity to hopefully stop Caden and bring her mother home.

When she arrived at the shop that morning, she felt more alive than ever. All day, her heart beat to an energetic rhythm. Despite feeling so anxious, she forced herself to maintain her bright smile and chipper voice for her customers while deep down her mind was racing, mentally preparing to confront the Dark Fairy—no, mentally preparing to confront *Caden*.

After work that day, she gobbled up one of her favorite cookies—a bright lemon sugar cookie with creamy blueberry frosting—and made her way to the castle.

She fluttered into the intimidating stone castle. The thick, massive doors slammed shut behind her, pushing her forward with a cool gust of wind. There was no turning back.

The Dark Fairy

Hovering a few inches off the ground, she moved down a great hall studded with bulky pillars that stretched from floor to ceiling. The walls were lined with portraits of fairies—not just any fairies, but the fairies who had disappeared. She saw some of her neighbors, and then she saw Finn, his fierce green eyes frozen with rage, Lyla, stunned with surprise, and her mother, her wide eyes glossy with tears.

When she got to her mom, she paused. A pain bloomed through her chest and her vision blurred as a mixture of intense sadness and anger washed through her small body. She so badly wanted to attack the Dark Fairy and get revenge for all the pain he had caused. Her hand slid down her side, feeling the smooth bottle of Dust by her waist, and she mentally prepared to use it if needed.

"Your mom was a good fairy," a dark voice rasped down the hall. Soft, scraping footsteps echoed off the tall walls.

Iris looked down the hall and saw the Dark Fairy

walking, not flying, from one of the side chambers to the hall's center. Iris landed, her small feet touching the cold stone floor, and craned her neck to look up at him.

"What did you do to her?" she asked.

His sunken eyes looked at her for a few seconds before he responded. "She was very kind, but not unlike the others."

Iris was about to ask what he meant by that, but then remembered her plan. She took a few deep breaths and then asked, "Caden, what happened to you?"

The Dark Fairy's eyes shifted slightly as if he was not expecting the question. "What do you mean?"

"You did so much for everyone," she said. "You could've kept your ability to collect Dust a secret, but instead, you taught all of us how to collect it for ourselves. Why?"

"Because I wanted to help everyone. I saw the benefit storing Dust provided, and I wanted

The Dark Fairy

everyone to experience it."

"Right," Iris said, stepping closer. "You did so much for everyone. What changed? What made you want to take it back?"

Caden peeled back the side of his dark cloak to reveal a bottle of Dust.

"I suggest you leave, fairy, before you end up like the others."

Iris's face grew warm as her fight-or-flight instincts kicked in. Taking a deep breath, she allowed herself a second to calm her nerves and then asked, "Why do you want me to leave?"

"Because I don't want to hurt you."

"Why would you hurt me?"

"Because..." Caden began, and then paused. After a second, he asked a different question. "What do you want? Are you going to ask me to return everything to the way it was?"

"No," Iris said, stepping closer. "I want to understand what happened to you."

"Why?" he asked sharply.

"Because," she replied. "You were one of the kindest and most generous fairies, and something changed. I can't imagine you changed on your own. Something caused that. I'm not leaving here until I understand what happened."

Caden popped the cork off his bottle, his eyes lowered to the ground.

"I'm giving you one last chance to leave," he said.

Iris's pulse quickened. She considered opening her own bottle, but she thought she detected some longing in his voice, as if somewhere deep inside he did not want to hurt her. So she forced herself to stay calm.

"I'm not going anywhere."

Caden sighed and, before she could react, flicked his hand up, and a stream of Dust rushed out of the bottle and hurtled towards the young fairy.

3

Unable to defend herself quickly enough, Iris squinted her eyes and looked away, bracing for impact.

But the impact never came.

Slowly, she peeled open her right eye, and then her left, and noticed the Dust wasn't meant to attack her—it instead formed a large translucent cloud between them. At first, all she could see inside the cloud were balls of white particles in varying densities, but then an image started to appear. As the image materialized, she recognized a younger version of Caden, before he'd transitioned into the Dark Fairy. As if being painted by an invisible brush, an

The Dark Fairy

environment slowly revealed itself inside the cloud around him.

Caden was sitting, initially appearing to float in midair, but dozens of blades of vibrant green grass began appearing beneath him. The grass spread, multiplying into hundreds and then thousands of soft blades that spread out and formed a hilltop. Blotches of color splashed above the grassy knoll to reveal six other fairies seated in a circle facing one another.

Iris recognized the fairies as Finn and the other village leaders. Was this one of Caden's memories?

Iris focused on Caden as he sat and listened to the others speak. A lump formed in her throat. Her skin prickled. She felt anxious. These feelings were not hers, she realized.

They were Caden's.

The leaders were discussing conflicts that had arisen as the fairies became bitter towards one another in their pursuit for Dust. They were

The Dark Fairy

developing a plan to divide up the land among the fairies—rules where each fairy would be allowed to farm Dust—when Caden straightened up to speak. After coughing to clear his throat, he said, "Excuse me, everyone, I think we're going about this the wrong way."

Finn turned to look at him. "What do you mean?"

"Trying to control fairies and restrict how they can farm Dust will only lead to more anger," Caden said. "Some fairies will get better land than others, jealousy will grow, and things will get worse."

"We can't just continue the way things are," another fairy, Zell, objected in a deep voice.

"I agree," Caden said. "Something needs to change. But I think there's a better—"

"We've been debating this for weeks," Zell continued. "We need to take action."

Caden felt his skin flush from being interrupted. He took a breath and then said, "I know. I'm not suggesting we don't take action. I just think…"

The Dark Fairy

"Zell's right," Finn interrupted. "We've been passive on this for too long."

Caden's yellow wings flickered quickly with frustration. "We aren't solving the root problem," he said. "We are trying to control a symptom of it. I have an idea I think could really make a difference."

Finn held up his hand, signaling for Caden to be silent. "I'm sorry, friend, I agree with the others on this one."

"But you haven't even heard my suggestion," Caden pleaded.

"I've made my decision," Finn said with finality. "We'll divide up the territory the way the others suggested. If things don't get better, we'll hash out your idea, Caden, and consider it then."

Suddenly, time rushed forward and the scene changed. The hill remained stationary, but the sky morphed from a cloudless late-afternoon day to a cloudy evening just after sunset. The same seven fairies were circled around the hill, but in different clothing and different positions. Several days or weeks had passed. No one was sitting this time. Each fairy was either standing and pacing back and forth or fluttering inches above the ground, zipping one way and then rushing back, their minds spinning too fast to be still.

"Things are getting bad," one of the fairies said. "Penna and Lyle got into a pretty nasty fight over a Dust cloud that appeared on the border of their territories."

"I caught someone gathering Dust from the middle of mine," another said.

"We need to create harsher penalties for trespassing," Zell demanded.

Caden, who was sitting next to Finn, turned to him and said, "Can I share my idea now?"

"We don't have time for that," one of the fairies objected.

"Right," Zell agreed. "Besides, we created

territories, and some fairies aren't respecting them. If we go back now and get rid of the territories instead of punishing them, no one will take any of our rules seriously."

"I'm not talking about creating more rules," Caden said. "I'm suggesting an entirely different—"

"Finn," another fairy interrupted, handing Finn a long, thin scroll of paper with writing on it, "The rest of us came up with suggestions for consequences for fairies who don't respect the territory boundaries. I'd imagine it will take a while for us to come to agreement on this, so I propose we start figuring this out immediately."

"I second that," another fairy said. The rest, save for Caden, all nodded their heads in agreement.

Finn glanced down at the scroll and read the first few words. He looked up at Caden with solemn eyes. "I'm sorry, friend. We need to see this through before we consider new solutions. We've gone too far to course correct."

The Dark Fairy

Caden opened his mouth to protest, but Finn turned and started reading the proposed new rules, ready to discuss them among the group.

As Iris watched, a sliver of darkness slowly materialized around Caden and start circling his body. Since no one reacted to it, it must have been invisible.

Defeated, Caden sat down on the grass to listen to the group, and then, as if a gust of wind blew it apart, the memory cloud scattered and faded, leaving Iris and the present-day Caden alone in the hall.

The Dark Fairy

The Dark Fairy

4

After blinking a few times, Iris adjusted her eyes and looked at Caden, noticing something different. He was still surrounded by the darkness, but instead of a nebulous smoke-like aura, some of the darkness was parsed into dense strands that wove up and down his body, slithering vipers that twisted around him like the single strand she'd seen in his memory.

"That was when it started," Caden said, his gaze on the floor, his breathing slow as he reflected on that memory. "I was so angry they wouldn't even give me the chance to speak."

"I'm sure if Finn knew how you felt, he wouldn't have—"

"But he did!" Caden interrupted, looking back up at her, anger returning to his voice. "He and the other fairies were too preoccupied with their own ideas. No one cared to hear mine."

Iris bit her tongue. She had misstepped. Caden was clearly being emotional, which required her to respond with emotion, not logic.

Emotion requires an emotional response, logic requires a logical response.

"I'm sorry," she said, and paused a second to let Caden's anger dissipate. "I… I could feel your frustration while looking at that memory. I imagine it was so hard feeling like you had something valuable to share that would help, only to be ignored."

The anger in Caden's narrow face dissipated, and he nodded slowly. "I cared about everyone so much. I knew what the issue was, why everyone was becoming so unhappy, and I had a solution to help. Our meetings used to be so much more collaborative,

The Dark Fairy

with everyone encouraging each other to participate. Once we got so preoccupied with Dust, it was as if we didn't care to hear what others were saying."

"I'm sorry, Caden," Iris said. "That must have been so difficult for you, seeing those previously cheerful gatherings turn sour overnight."

Caden's eyes shut as he thought. Iris opened her mouth to say something, but decided to be silent until he was ready. *'Let the silence speak,'* she thought.

After a few moments, he opened his eyes.

"So we agreed on various punishments for fairies who broke the rules, and then we parted," he said flatly.

He seemed to be less emotional and more logical, so Iris felt she could get more logical with her questions.

"What was that black thing that started floating around you during that memory?" she asked. "There are several of them moving around you now."

"I don't know," Caden said. "They've been

The Dark Fairy

accumulating over time since that day. I don't know what it is, but it's more than just something hovering around me. I feel it. It's heavy, so heavy. It pulls down on my chest, compresses against my lungs, clouds my mind. The more there are, the harder it is to think and breathe."

"Did those slivers of darkness only appear during those meetings?"

"No," Caden said.

"Can you show me a time when one appeared in a different setting?"

Caden's eyes shifted slightly upward as he scanned his memories for such a time. When he found it, he looked back at the young cookie-maker and waved his hand. As some Dust left the bottle by his waist, a new memory cloud appeared. Blotches of color splashed into its midst, forming wooden planks along the ground and cabin-like walls along the edges. Burning orange flames inside a fireplace appeared next, followed by a dark wooden table and

The Dark Fairy

chairs with a large fiery lantern hanging from the ceiling overhead, its flickering light illuminating the room.

It was Caden's old house.

Caden was looking out the window. Iris's chest suddenly felt heavy as it filled with sadness and loneliness.

The wooden door in Caden's old house suddenly swung open, and a fairy she recognized as Hugo came charging in. Hugo's round eyes widened when he saw Caden, and he immediately rushed towards him and wrapped his massive arms around Caden's slender frame, squeezing so tightly Caden's back cracked a few times.

"All right, all right," Caden gasped under Hugo's embrace.

Hugo released Caden and looked at him with a larger-than-life smile, his leathery copper skin and tousled black hair glowing under the lantern's warm light. Though Hugo's lips formed a smile, his eyes

The Dark Fairy

told a different story—something bothered him.

Caden smiled and nodded as he recovered his breath. "It's good to see you too, Hugo."

"Caden," Hugo said. "How are you?" Caden opened his lips to respond, but before he could answer, Hugo continued. "I was hoping you could show me some new techniques for capturing wild Dust. I'm typically only able to get about half inside the bottle before the rest disappears."

Iris's chest felt heavier in the silence after he spoke.

"Hugo," Caden said. "I want to tell you something."

"Go for it!" Hugo said, clasping his hands together by his chest as if ready to take on a challenge.

"Hugo… I'm very sad."

Hugo laughed and spread his hands in shock. "What?! How can you be sad? Look at everything you've done! Everyone in the village looks up to you."

"But no one is happy, Hugo. Ever since we started

storing Dust, that's all anyone seems to care about. Yes, all the villagers look up to me now, but I've never felt so alone. I feel like the others don't want to actually talk to me, they just want me to teach them how to collect more Dust."

"Look at all the good Dust is providing, though."

"How do you feel, though?" Caden asked. "Right now?"

"I feel great," Hugo said in a voice that sound forced.

"Look me in the eyes and speak from your heart," Caden said.

Hugo regarded him for a moment as if gathering the energy to convince Caden he was good, but then he gave out a sigh and let his gaze fall to the floor. "You're right, I have been better. I'm just frustrated because I'm not able to collect as much Dust as others."

"It's more than that," Caden said. "I think you feel alone, probably a little unseen as well. Remember those *latías* we had in the past? Remember? Almost once a month, we got together to celebrate. I can't think of the last time we did that."

Hugo looked up at Caden. "We don't need those anymore because of you."

"How can you say we don't need those anymore? Those were the best times we had to get to know each other better, to talk, to laugh, to have fun."

"We're talking right now."

"Yes," Caden said. "But you didn't come here just to talk. You came here to learn how to collect more Dust."

Hugo's chipper voice started to weaken. "Caden, you're looking at this wrong. You're the best at collecting Dust. You can have and make whatever scenery you want, express yourself however you want. The rest of us want what you already have."

"But I'm telling you I'm in a lot of pain right now."

"You're just being overly sensitive," Hugo said.

The Dark Fairy

"It's all in your head."

"Does that make it any less real?"

Hugo sighed, his tone now completely somber. "Look, I need to gather some more Dust before nightfall or my home will start to revert back, so I don't have a lot of time right now. Will you please help me get better at collecting Dust, and then we can set up a time later to discuss this?"

"I will help you," Caden said, "but I want to tell you something. I think I know why everyone is unhappy, and I know how to fix—"

"Caden," Hugo interrupted, clearly getting frustrated. "I told you why I'm unhappy. I don't need a lecture. Are you going to help me or not?"

Looking into the vision, Iris noticed another sliver of darkness slowly materialize around Caden and start circling his body. After a pause, Caden nodded and said, "Okay, Hugo, I'll help you."

The memory cloud faded.

The Dark Fairy

The Dark Fairy

5

As Iris's eyes adjusted back to the present, she noticed that even more of the dense aura around Caden had refined into a multitude of dark strings that swirled around his body.

"No one listened to you." she said after a moment of silence. Caden didn't respond. "You were sad everyone was so focused on Dust and genuine friendships were breaking. You even had an idea to fix it, but no one would pay attention."

"Yes, that's right," Caden said.

"So why," Iris began, stepping even closer, "did you turn on everyone? I can understand you feeling sad and alone, but what made you want to lock yourself up in this castle and darken the land?"

Caden considered her words. Iris noticed that his demeanor had changed since they began their conversation. His anger was replaced with sadness and tenderness. He seemed calmer, more open.

"It was during my speech," Caden said. "Something happened then. I don't fully understand it. Something changed inside me, something took control."

"What was it?" Iris asked eagerly.

"I don't know," Caden said. "I can't explain it."

"Will you show me?"

He paused and looked at her, taking a breath.

"I haven't revisited this memory since it happened," he said. "I'm not sure what will happen to me if I relive it. Are you sure you want to see it?"

"I'm sure, Caden. I really want to understand what happened to you."

Caden closed his eyes a second. "Very well. This is the last memory I'll share."

6

Another wave of his hand, and a new memory cloud formed, presenting the scene when Caden addressed the villagers right before his transformation into the Dark Fairy. Iris instantly felt a rush of anxiety in her chest when she saw Caden about to speak.

"Friends," Caden said in the memory, "I want to share something with all of you." Everyone waited calmly to hear what he had to say.

"It's been a little over a year since we've been accumulating Dust," he continued. "This has allowed us to transform our pastures into brilliant works of art with running water, bright colors, and exotic fauna. All of that really brought our village to life and allowed us to communicate in ways beyond mere words. We have created something special."

There were some murmurs of appreciation, but most of the fairies seemed on edge.

"But I feel," Caden said, "like something even more precious has been deteriorating and is nearly lost."

Silence fell as all of the fairies focused on Caden.

"We have all become so consumed with Dust that it's all we talk about, all we seem to care about. We don't listen to each other anymore. Truly listen, I mean. It's as if in every conversation we have, we have a goal, something we want to get out of it. Everything we say or do during that conversation is to achieve that goal, regardless of how the other feels or what the other wants.

"Our land is more beautiful than ever, but we—*I* feel more alone than ever. I fear when it comes time for us to pass on, we won't be surrounded by loved ones and memories of deep relationships and life experiences, but instead we'll have a bunch of Dust in a cabinet and some flowers."

Caden took a deep breath before continuing.

"While I think accumulating Dust is good, we need to put a pause on it to re-focus on genuinely caring about one another." An uneasiness crept into Caden's words as he continued. "Therefore, I have decided to stop producing bottles and stop teaching Dust-collecting until we restore our community to how we were before."

There was a long silence. Finally, one of the fairies said, "Caden, with all due respect, you have more Dust than all of us combined. To tell us you want to stop making bottles and helping us just means you will be the only one to benefit from the Dust."

"I'll release all my Dust back into the wild," Caden said quickly.

"We need the Dust," another fairy said with a touch of desperation. "Our land is so much more

The Dark Fairy

colorful and vibrant now. You're just trying to control us."

Caden was about to respond, but another fairy spoke first.

"Yeah, you can't punish the rest of us because of your feelings. You need to change your mindset and be more optimistic."

"No," Caden said, his face growing hot as he became defensive. "I'm not just talking about my feelings. Don't you all feel similarly?" As he spoke, Iris noticed another black strand materialize and start whirling around him.

It seemed as if some of the audience were considering what he had just said, some even starting to agree.

"Of course not," Finn scoffed, standing tall, puffing his chest. "Look at everything we've built. Sure, there are challenges, but we're building something great. Isn't that right?" Finn looked around the audience, and a wave of agreement slowly passed through them.

"Stop focusing on what you can see with your eyes," Caden said. "What about what you feel in your hearts?"

"Your emotions are clouding your perspective," a bespectacled fairy said. Another strand of darkness appeared around Caden, adding itself to the writhing pattern of black that covered his body.

On and on it went, Caden trying to explain his concerns and the villagers telling him why he was wrong. Every time a fairy attacked him and every time his message went unheard, more black threads appeared around his body, invisible to the audience but in plain sight of Iris as she viewed the memory.

Suddenly, Iris's skin prickled as she watched the black strands around Caden start multiplying faster than ever. They swirled around his body quicker and quicker, blinding his vision, deafening his thoughts. Suffocating him. Iris felt it difficult to breathe—she had to take deeper and deeper breaths to get an even smaller amount of air. The audience continued talking, but she could not make out their words. She couldn't focus on anything other than struggling to suck air into her lungs.

Caden fell to his knees as the darkness closed in on him. A searing pain jolted throughout his body as if lightning had struck his nerves. He screamed as his skin charred from ivory to a ghostly pale, his blue eyes blackened, his unkempt hair elongated, straightened, and became jet black. The strings of darkness suddenly snapped towards Caden and impaled his body, driving through him like a lance through a foe. Iris turned her head and squeezed her eyes shut as a dark shockwave radiated out from Caden, temporarily blacking out everything in the memory.

When Iris opened her eyes, the darkness had faded, revealing the memory once more. She noticed the familiar cloud-like aura around him, visible for everyone to see. She no longer felt sadness or

The Dark Fairy

loneliness. She no longer felt anything.

The darkness had taken over.

The Dark Fairy

The Dark Fairy

7

The audience was frozen in fright as they watched Caden on his knees, head hung low, panting heavily. When his breathing settled, his darkened wings started fluttering as he rose into the air. He lifted his head to face the audience. Some of the fairies gasped when he opened his sunken eyes in a glare.

"This meeting is over," the Dark Fairy said, Caden's once concerned and thoughtful voice replaced by a deep, raspy sound. "From this day forward, no fairies are allowed to collect or use Dust. If you do, I will vanish you."

He held up his hand, and fairies screamed as bottles of Dust were summoned out of their homes, breaking through glass and blasting through wood as they gathered above the Dark Fairy.

As the memory cloud started to fade, Iris felt Caden's emptiness. He felt pure hatred, liquid rage. His thoughts were not his; they belonged to the darkness.

The memory vanished.

Iris gasped when she looked up at Caden and saw he was no longer standing on the ground. He was floating in the air about halfway between the stone floor and the wide, arched ceiling. The dark aura was bigger than ever, pulsing with a heartbeat of its own, full of hundreds of black strands that spun around his body rapidly, much as they had during his speech.

"Enough!" the Dark Fairy yelled in a deep voice. "You have seen enough."

"Caden!" Iris called, realizing the darkness was taking over again. "I understand!"

The Dark Fairy raised his lifeless hand, his

The Dark Fairy

blackened palm facing the ceiling. A stream of Dust left his bottle and formed a ball inches above his palm.

"For so long," Iris yelled up at him, "you tried sharing your feelings with everyone. Your sadness because fairies only spoke with you to collect more Dust. Your isolation because you felt your friendships were becoming artificial. Your fear that bonds between everyone were deteriorating, and your anger that no one would listen to you."

As she spoke, some of the darkness around him started to fade, but that only caused the remaining darkness to move faster and more violently.

"Your time is ending," the deep voice echoed.

"You gave so much," Iris said, tears starting to fall from her eyes and roll down her cheeks. "You trained everyone on how to collect Dust. You spent so much of your time giving without asking for anything in return. You helped so many people, Caden. And when you just wanted to be heard, to be understood, everyone turned their backs on you."

More of the darkness began to fade.

"I'm so sorry you had to deal with that. I can't imagine how painful that was."

"Silence!" the Dark Fairy bellowed as he flicked his hand forward. The Dust hurtled towards Iris in a flash—

Iris uncorked the bottle about her waist and flung its contents into the air in front of her just before the Dust struck.

A massive impact from Dust colliding into Dust blasted Iris off her feet and several yards down the hallway, crashing to the hard floor. She lost her breath as she landed on her back with a thud. Too weak to stand, she propped herself up on her elbows as the Dark Fairy hovered closer until he was nearly directly overhead. She watched as he prepared a new ball of Dust.

This time, she had no defense.

"Caden," Iris said weakly. "You had a right to feel

The Dark Fairy

everything you did. You were trying so hard to help everyone find their happiness again, and when no one listened to you and dismissed your feelings, you felt suffocated, like you couldn't breathe, like you couldn't get air."

The Dark Fairy's body started to shake, and though more of the aura faded, the remaining darkness seemed to become more persistent, latching onto his skin and forcing his body to move under its own will.

"All you wanted..." Iris continued, protectively holding her hand over her chest, "was to be heard."

"Ahhh..." Caden's voice came through the darkness. "You...." he struggled to speak, clearly fighting to regain control. "You... understand!" he shouted.

The darkness instantly impaled his body just as it had done during his speech. Still hovering in the air, Caden hunched over, screaming in pain as the darkness shot through him, engulfing him from the inside out. Then, with a swift motion, he flung himself upright and arched his back, his ball of Dust dissolving into the air.

Iris shielded her eyes as a massive black shockwave exploded from his body. The darkness poured out of him like a reservoir through a broken dam, forceful and chaotic. Several more shockwaves followed as the murky blackness gushed from his body until he seemed empty. As the darkness bled from Caden, his hair shortened and returned to its brown hue, his wings regained their yellow color, and his eyes brightened.

When the shockwaves finally stopped, Caden descended to the ground as if he were falling in slow motion. When he landed, he dropped to his knee, supporting himself with one hand, gazing down as he gathered his breath. He appeared mentally and physically drained, but he also appeared calm.

As Iris lowered her hand protecting her eyes, she noticed the residual darkness coil uselessly along the floor before it finally faded into nothingness. It was gone.

She looked at Caden intently, unsure what to say, unsure what to feel.

Eventually, he tilted his head to look at her and pulled himself to his feet. Wincing as he walked, he slowly moved towards her. When he reached her, he extended his hand down to help her stand. Nervous at first, Iris feebly raised her arm, allowing him to grab her hand and assist her to her feet.

"Iris," Caden said as he regained his breath, his voice calm and gentle once more. "Thank you. From the bottom of my heart, thank you for listening to me."

She looked into his blue eyes, no longer darkened or saddened, and smiled. "You're welcome, Caden."

After a moment, he stepped back, his eyes scanning the great hall.

"I feel," he said, "like I can breathe again." He closed his eyes and took a deep breath. "Ah, I have longed for this feeling for so long. It feels so nice."

Iris's heartbeat settled as she let Caden reflect in the silence.

"You must be wondering about your mother," Caden said, and then opened his eyes to look at her.

"Yes," she said. "The other villagers said she was dead, but I don't believe you killed all these fairies."

"No," Caden said, "I didn't. The darkness compelled me to punish them, but I wasn't so far lost as to want to kill them or cause them pain. They were frozen in time and transformed into those portraits you saw along the hall when you entered. They're asleep, free from pain. Allow me to wake them."

Caden waved his hand, and Dust flew out of his bottle, splitting into several horizontal columns that funneled into each portrait. One by one the portraits burst to life, and the fairies were restored. Finn, Lyla, her mother, and the others looked around as they sprung back to life, trying to understand what had happened. Iris couldn't contain herself and

The Dark Fairy

immediately pounced on her mother (nearly knocking her over), embracing her tightly as tears streamed from her eyes.

The Dark Fairy

The Dark Fairy

8

As the fairies came to their senses, Iris and Caden explained what had happened. The fairies certainly were not happy with what Caden had done to them, and Caden agreed to accept whatever punishment they deemed fair. He assured them he would return their bottles and do whatever he could to make up for his actions.

Everyone was anxious to see their families again, so the fairies left the castle—with the exception of Iris. After saying farewell to the others, she turned back to speak with Caden, but he had left the hall.

She wandered through the castle, eventually finding him upstairs out on a balcony overlooking the

The Dark Fairy

village. He rested his arms on the wooden rail and gazed out, watching as all the bottles of Dust flew through the air, returning to their former owners.

Iris walked up beside him. She was too short to see over the rail, so she popped up in the air, her bright green wings fluttering as she lifted herself up and then settled down to sit on the smooth rail beside him.

"What are you still doing here?" Caden asked her curiously.

"I have a question for you," she said. "Do you think collecting Dust is bad? Would we be better off if we didn't do it?"

Caden considered her words for a while before answering.

"No, I don't think it's bad. Collecting Dust has allowed us to make something special and express ourselves. We just need to ensure that we don't get so self-absorbed that we stop caring for and listening to others. Which is not easy."

Caden paused and then pointed out at some of the villagers in the distance.

"Look," he said. "Can you see the darkness around them?"

Iris looked out and noticed that most of the fairies had a small dark aura about them. Previously, she had seen it around just a few fairies, but now practically everyone did.

"Did that just happen?"

"No," Caden said. "You just haven't noticed it until now. That darkness comes from the need to be heard. We all have a deep craving to be understood. In most conversations, fairies prioritize talking over listening, and when they do listen, they typically listen with the intent to respond, not to actually understand. As this craving builds and fewer fairies listen to each other, the darkness comes, and it's as if we lack air to breathe.

"Take our conversation right now. You probably aren't thinking about air at all, and you're able to fully listen to me. But what if all the air around us suddenly vanished? Then that's all you would think about, and you couldn't pay attention to a single word I spoke."

"Hmm," Iris considered his words. "So when we don't listen to others, it's as if we are robbing them of their air? All they can think about is getting us to understand them so they can breathe again. Anything we're trying to say in the meantime gets lost."

"Exactly," Caden said. "By actually listening to others and showing them we understand, we give them back their air. Once they can breathe, they can listen. Only then can we have a truly meaningful conversation."

"So how can we show others we understand?" Iris asked. "How do we listen?"

Caden reflected on how Iris had vanquished his own darkness. "I felt like you truly understood when you explained my situation in your own words while

The Dark Fairy

also labeling the emotions I felt. You described my situation: that I gave so much of my time helping others collect Dust, only to be ignored when I shared my concerns. And then you described my feelings: that I felt sadness and isolation at first, fear for where we were heading, and then anger at being ignored. The only way you would have been able to say those things was by actually listening to me and understanding. That made me feel visible."

Iris nodded. "So, repeat back to them in my own words what they are trying to communicate to me and label their feelings?"

"Yes," Caden answered. "That is how to truly show someone you're listening."

"Isn't that kind of weird?" Iris asked. "Repeating back what someone just told me makes it sound robotic."

Caden laughed. "Well, if you just repeated word for word what they said, then yes, I'd agree. But you'd be surprised how often you *think* you know what someone is trying to say but you don't, despite it sounding obvious. More often than not, when I rephrase and repeat back to someone what they just told me, they tell me I didn't understand them correctly.

"When that happens, they explain it differently, and I repeat it back until they tell me I understand. If I didn't take the time to repeat back what I heard, we would move forward without understanding each other, and the root of almost all conflicts can be boiled down to misunderstandings."

"Ahh," Iris said. "That makes sense."

"The key is rephrasing what they said in your own words," Caden continued. "That's impossible to do unless you were truly listening. When someone uses their own words to explain how we're feeling and why we're feeling that way, it's magical. We feel cleansed, like one of our deepest yearnings has been fulfilled. Because it has."

The two looked out at the villagers again. Iris saw

all the fairies moving about, not talking or laughing, simply moving about the land, their minds preoccupied and their hearts quiet. The darkness followed them everywhere they went.

'Rephrase and repeat back to them in my own words what they just said and label their feelings,' Iris reminded herself.

"Well, Caden," she said, hopping off the rail, "We have some work to do."

Caden stepped away from the rail and smiled. "Yes. Yes, I suppose we do."

The Dark Fairy

The Dark Fairy

A Note from the Author

I hope you enjoyed this story.

Almost all of us have a deep yearning to be understood. Unfortunately, listening is a rare skill. We are told in school, "You have two ears and one mouth for a reason," but beyond that, we aren't really taught the importance of listening or even how to do it.

As a business owner, brother, son, friend, and mentor, I am constantly amazed at how powerful listening is when I am interacting with others. So many epiphanies have materialized between me and someone else when I have stopped to truly and deeply listen. Done properly, listening can be extraordinarily healing.

That being said, listening is hard. Sometimes, it can be *very* hard. The mental strength required to deeply listen is intense. There are times when someone else is talking and every ounce of me wants to interrupt and interject my viewpoint. It takes a lot of effort and patience to listen well. Every time I do it, though, the struggle is worth it.

Here are some quick tips on listening.

Let Them Breathe

Not feeling understood can feel suffocating, like you can't breathe. If your counterpart feels suffocated, she likely won't pay much attention to what you have to say.

View it as your mission to remove your counterpart's suffocation so she can breathe as quickly as possible, and you'll be surprised how quickly the argument will dissolve and turn into a positive, productive conversation. You can do this by making her feel understood.

Rephrase and Label Emotions

To show someone we understand her, we should repeat back what she said in our own words, essentially summarizing what she just said. If there are emotions tied to what she said, we should also label those emotions.

For example, if someone just got done venting about how much she hates her job because she doesn't feel challenged and does the same thing over and over, I could say something like, "So it sounds like you are really unhappy at work because you don't feel like you're learning or growing. Is that right?"

Ask Questions vs Making Statements

Conversations are fluid, and it may not always be apparent how you can repeat something back to the other person and label their emotion. When this happens, ask questions such as:

Can you explain what you meant when you said ___?

Can you tell me more about ___?

Why did you feel ___ when that happened?

Questions like those invite the other person to sift through their thoughts and expand, helping you, and even themselves, truly understand how they're feeling.

Try to Get the Other Person to Say "That's Right"

Whenever someone says "That's right" to something you've said, you have reached clarity and understanding. Keep rephrasing and repeating back what the other person says, label emotions, and ask questions to gain understanding until the other person says, "Yes, that's right."

Resist the Urge to Defend or Problem-Solve

Two types of conversations in which listening is incredibly important are arguments and conversations dealing with problems.

During an argument, your counterpart is likely expressing thoughts that can be perceived as attacks. Our initial instinct is to defend ourselves or share our perspective, but before we do, it is important we make our counterpart feel heard. If some of my team members just got done telling me they feel I prioritize making money over their safety in the workplace, my initial instinct is to immediately defend myself and tell them why they're wrong. However, first I need to give them air to breathe. Responding like

The Dark Fairy

this is much more effective:

"To make sure I heard you correctly, it sounds like based on a few decisions I've made over the past couple of months, you think I am focused more on making money than the team's safety, and it's making you feel unhappy and unsafe at work. Is that right?"

Assuming they agree (which is already a huge step towards finding common ground), I'd continue with:

"Okay, I understand where you're coming from, and I'm very sorry I made you all feel that way. I value your safety significantly more than money. Without you as my team, the company wouldn't exist. If it's okay with you, I'd like to walk through the examples you shared of decisions I've made, explain my point of view on them, and then hear from you how I could've acted differently to not make you feel unsafe. Is that all right with you?"

After saying something like this, the hostility will likely have dissipated, no one is in a defending posture, and we can talk through the issues on the same side of the table vs opposing sides.

During a conversation dealing with problems, most people's initial reaction is to start problem-solving. This usually isn't good for two reasons. First, if you do this, you haven't given yourself a chance to truly understand the problem you're trying to solve. Second, if the other person doesn't feel you understand the problem he's communicating, he won't be very receptive to your suggestions.

Many times, the initial problem identified is a symptom of a deeper root cause, and time spent treating symptoms vs root causes isn't very effective. For example, someone may express they are unhappy with their job. If I immediately try to solve this problem, I may focus on helping him update his resume and look for a new job. However, if instead I keep reflecting and labeling, the conversation could go something like this:

The Dark Fairy

HIM: *"I've been a funk lately because I'm so miserable at work. Something needs to change."*

ME: *"I'm sorry to hear that. It sounds like work is making you unhappy, so you want a change like getting a new job?"*

HIM: *"Well, no, I like the company I work for. I was hired to do digital marketing, but I'm spending all my time focusing on internal communications."*

ME: *"So you're frustrated you aren't doing what you were hired to do?"*

HIM: *"Not just that, but I got my degree in digital marketing and that's my passion."*

ME: *"Oh, so you want to stay with your current company, but you just aren't doing work you're passionate about. Sounds like you need to find a way to switch to the digital marketing department. Is that right?"*

The Dark Fairy

HIM: *"Yes, exactly."*

The root cause is not just that he dislikes his job; it's that he is not using his passion of digital marketing. The problem-solving can begin now. We should focus on what he needs to do to get transferred to a new department, *not* updating his resume and looking for new jobs.

Whenever the conversation deals with an argument or someone bringing up a problem, resist the urge to defend or problem-solve. Listen by reflecting, labeling, and asking questions until the other person confirms you understand.

Have Patience

Nearly every time I empathetically listen to people and repeat back to them what they just said, they correct me.

The Dark Fairy

Many times when they correct me, they are either introducing new information or going against something they just said. Sometimes I feel a flash of frustration because it appears like they are changing their story.

Our minds are curious things. We may think and believe one thing, but when we hear someone repeat it back to us, it sounds different than we thought. We change our mind, and that's okay. In fact, that's better than okay. When this happens, we are helping the other person clarify her thoughts, which can be very cleansing.

Respond to Emotions with Emotion and Logic with Logic

When someone is expressing emotions, don't respond back with logic. Instead, identify and label his emotions so he feels you understand. If you respond with logic, he will likely not be receptive and will argue with you because he feels you don't fully understand his perspective.

When someone is speaking logically, now is the time to respond with logic.

A typical conversation will switch back and forth between logical and emotional discussions, almost like a dance. By staying in sync with your counterpart, you'll keep progressing forward.

Conclusion

I encourage you to challenge yourself in the next in-depth disagreement you have with someone to truly listen and make him feel understood. No matter how stubborn or angry the other person sounds, remember that he is just suffocating from not feeling understood.

There is likely a darkness inside him, and just like with Caden, that darkness is preventing him from being calm and rational. Like Iris, all you have to do is listen. It won't always be easy; sometimes it will be the hardest thing you ever do.

But it will be worth it. I promise.

The Dark Fairy

Request for You

I would really appreciate any feedback you have on this book, and it would mean a lot to me if you left a helpful review on Amazon sharing your thoughts.

My next story is one about managing others. My aim is to focus on soft skills applicable both in life and business and showing them through a fun, engaging story. If you would like to be notified of future book releases, please subscribe to my newsletter by going to www.nickleja.com.

Also - if there are any soft skills you feel are not taught in schools or that others could benefit from knowing, please let me know. I'd love to learn about

The Dark Fairy

new skills and distill them into a fun story everyone can read. You can share any ideas by going to my website.

Thank you so much for reading The Dark Fairy!

About the Author

Nick Leja opened his first business shortly after graduating college. Since then, he has continued to open and invest in businesses and real estate across the country in a variety of industries.

His passion is helping others grow by sharing his knowledge through reading and personal experiences. Trying to avoid getting "stuck" with being an adult, daydreaming is one of his favorite hobbies, and writing allows him to fuse his creativity with business in a way to have fun and help others.

The Dark Fairy

The Dark Fairy

The Dark Fairy

The Dark Fairy

The Dark Fairy

The Dark Fairy

The Dark Fairy

Made in the USA
Coppell, TX
03 November 2022